My
Little Book of
ANIMAL
ADVENTURES

This book belongs to:

_____

Published by Sequoia Children's Publishing,
a division of Phoenix International Publications, Inc.

8501 West Higgins Road, Suite 790
Chicago, Illinois 60631

59 Gloucester Place
London W1U 8JJ

© 2019 Sequoia Publishing & Media, LLC

www.sequoiakidsbooks.com

10 9 8 7 6 5 4 3 2 1

ISBN 978-1-64269-073-6

Contents

Farm Puppy

Written by Lenaya Raack
Illustrated by Deborah Colvin Borgo

In a corner of the barn, four tiny puppies snuggle against Mother Dog's side. They are four days old. Mother Dog made a bed for them away from the clucking hens, away from the curious piglets, and away from the busy farmer.

The tiny puppies sleep most of the day. They cannot see, they cannot hear, and they cannot walk. The puppies need Mother Dog to take care of them.

Every day the puppies drink Mother Dog's milk, and Mother Dog gives her babies a bath. And every night Father Dog sleeps near them. During the day, he helps the farmer take care of his sheep.

Farm Puppy

Farm Puppy

The farmer watches one of the puppies explore the barn. His name is Farm Puppy, and he is three weeks old now. He can see and hear all the animals who live in the barn. He hears the rooster crow every morning. He sees the brown hen sitting on her eggs. He hears the piglets squealing as they play. And he sees the brown cow eating the hay.

Today, Farm Puppy visits the baby chicks. Farm Puppy wants to round up the chicks. He walks in a circle around the chicks, trying to move them to the back of the barn. When Farm Puppy comes too close, the chicks run and hide under Mother Hen's feathers. Mother Hen squawks at Farm Puppy, and he runs back to Mother Dog.

The bright sun shines on the barnyard. It is springtime! Farm Puppy is five weeks old. He likes to watch his mother and father herd the sheep. Father Dog herds the sheep through a gate. Mother Dog chases after a sheep that is running away. Soon Farm Puppy will be able to herd sheep, too. But for now, he practices with other barnyard animals.

Farm Puppy runs over to the chickens, but they keep eating. He races over to Mother Pig and her piglets. Mother Pig just snorts at Farm Puppy. She doesn't want anyone near her piglets. Farm Puppy runs over to the calves but they are eating, too. No one seems to listen to Farm Puppy.

Farm Puppy

Now Farm Puppy is six weeks old. He finally gets to help the farmer, Mother Dog, and Father Dog take the sheep to the pasture! Farm Puppy follows Mother and Father Dog as they move the sheep out of the farm gate. The farmer blows his whistle and moves his hands. When the farmer moves his hand, Father Dog walks around the sheep. When the farmer whistles, Mother Dog barks at the sheep and makes them move.

Now Farm Puppy plays follow the leader. When Mother Dog runs after a sheep, Farm Puppy runs after the sheep, too. When Father Dog lies down and stares at the sheep, so does Farm Puppy. This is good practice for being a sheepdog!

Farm Puppy

Farm Puppy has been exploring the pasture while the sheep eat. It is hot in the sun. Farm Puppy looks for some water to drink. In the corner of the pasture, he finds a pond. Farm Puppy bends his head to take a drink. Suddenly, he sees a strange dog in the water! Farm Puppy lies on the ground and stares. But the dog has gone away. Farm Puppy stands up again. He sees the dog again!

Then Farm Puppy barks at the strange dog. The other dog barks, too. Farm Puppy circles the pond and runs toward the dog and then—splash! Farm Puppy is all wet. The farmer rescues the puppy and takes him back to the herd.

Farm Puppy

Farm Puppy is staying home today. He likes to play in the barnyard. Farm Puppy walks up to the geese, and stares at them. He is trying to herd them into the barn. But the geese just stare back! When they walk away from the barn, Farm Puppy tries to stop them. He circles them and barks loudly.

Honk! Honk! The geese run in all different directions! Farm Puppy races after them, into the squawking chickens, over the hay bales, through the legs of the mooing calves, under the fence and back again. Then they fly on top of a hay wagon. Farm Puppy stops and barks. But they will not come down. And they will not go into the barn. Herding is hard work!

Suddenly Farm Puppy hears another kind of honk. The children have come home on the school bus! Farm Puppy races to meet them. The bus starts to move, but it is too fast for Farm Puppy to catch.

"Here, Puppy!" the children yell. Farm Puppy runs to them as they walk toward the house. But Farm Puppy doesn't want them to go into the house. He circles the children. The children stop.

"Puppy must think we are some kind of funny sheep," the boy says. When Farm Puppy sits and stares, the children start walking. When Farm Puppy stands and barks, they stop. Finally they tell Farm Puppy to sit and be a good dog.

Farm Puppy

Farm Puppy

Just then, Farm Puppy hears the farmer's whistle. The farmer is calling him! Farm Puppy is now six months old. The farmer must teach Farm Puppy to be a good sheepdog. They practice every day. Farm Puppy learns what to do when the farmer whistles and moves his hands.

Farm Puppy learns how to take the sheep out the gate and bring them back in again. Farm Puppy learns to move the sheep so that he is on one side of them and the farmer is on the other. The farmer teaches Farm Puppy what to do when a sheep runs away. Farm Puppy learns very fast. Soon Farm Puppy will be able to move the sheep like his mother and father.

Today, Farm Puppy and Father Dog are in the pasture with the sheep. The sky darkens as rain begins to fall. Thunder sounds, and the farmer decides it's time to take the sheep back to the farm.

The sheep are afraid. They start to run away. Farm Puppy circles the sheep like his father. The farmer signals. Now Farm Puppy and Father Dog must turn the sheep. The sheep head for the farm.

When the thunder roars again, one lamb runs away. Farm Puppy runs after it. Father Dog and the farmer take the sheep back to the farm. They wait for Farm Puppy to come home with the lamb.

Farm Puppy

Finally, the farmer and Father Dog go looking for them. There is no sign of Farm Puppy or the lamb. Father Dog barks. Then Farm Puppy barks back. The farmer and Father Dog run to Farm Puppy. They find Farm Puppy and the lamb. The lamb is stuck in mud. The farmer pulls him out. He pats Farm Puppy and tells him that he is the best sheepdog.

Baby Penguin

Written by Jennifer Boudart
Illustrated by Lori Nelson Field

Ark! Ark! At the frozen seaside, the penguins greet each other with a loud barking noise. Father Penguin returns from a swim in the sea. He builds up speed until he can leap out of the water and land on the ice. Then he shakes the water off his feathers. It is now Father Penguin's turn to stay close to the nest so Mother Penguin can go fishing.

Mother Penguin climbs from the nest. Her movements wake her baby. Baby Penguin blinks her bright black eyes.

Baby Penguin

Baby Penguin

Baby Penguin is a slowpoke. When she was born, she took half a day to break out of her shell. It takes a long time for her to eat, too. And even though she is three weeks old, she has never left her nest.

Baby Penguin looks around. Penguins are everywhere, and they are all squawking loudly! They sure are noisy.

Penguins are birds, but they cannot fly. Baby Penguin's wings are really more like flippers. Although she'll never fly in the sky like other birds, Baby Penguin will be able to fly through the water with her special wings.

Each family of penguins guards its nest. If a stranger gets too close, Father Penguin stretches his neck. His neck feathers fluff out. He points his head up to the sky and grunts. Baby Penguin stretches her neck and grunts, too.

Father Penguin and his baby tell the stranger to keep away from their home.

Father Penguin protected Baby Penguin when she was just an egg, too. He held the egg on top of his feet so it wouldn't touch the ice for almost two months. A flap of warm belly skin covered the egg and kept it warm. Baby Penguin is lucky to have Father Penguin!

Baby Penguin

Baby Penguin

Mother and Father Penguin must go fishing often to catch enough food for their tiny baby. They will have to leave her for a while. Baby Penguin's mother and father bring her to a group of young penguins. She slowly waddles after them.

Baby Penguin will be safe in this group. The older penguins will watch for danger. They circle around the babies and shelter them from cold winds.

If an enemy approaches the babies, the adult penguins will beat their wings and screech, scaring the enemy away.

Baby Penguin snuggles with the others. She falls asleep. Baby Penguin does not notice the group moving away from her. She wakes up and sees a bird diving at her!

Luckily, an older penguin is nearby. The big penguin runs toward Baby Penguin, waving his flippers and barking loudly. He scares the bird, and it flies away!

Baby Penguin hasn't learned how to escape danger, yet. Soon Mother and Father Penguin will teach her how to swim really fast through the water and away from danger.

Baby Penguin

34

Baby Penguin

Baby Penguin goes back to the other penguins. She is frightened and very hungry. Suddenly she hears her father calling to her! Will he find her? Baby Penguin is lost in a crowd of fuzzy little black penguins that look just like her.

Baby Penguin lifts her head and barks as loudly as she can. Her parents hear her over all the other noise. They find her!

Baby Penguin is happy to return to the nest with Mother and Father Penguin. She knows it is time for them to feed her the fish that they have caught in the sea.

Penguins get all of their food from the ocean. They eat fish, crab, and squid. They also eat small sea creatures called plankton. Penguins have spiky tongues that help them grip the slippery fish in their beaks.

When penguins get thirsty, they can eat snow to quench their thirst. And they can drink salty ocean water without getting sick.

After Baby Penguin eats her meal, Mother and Father Penguin "clean house." They replace the rocks that have tumbled off their nest pile.

Baby Penguin

A snowstorm has blown in from the ocean.
Large, white flakes are falling everywhere. Baby Penguin
is lucky to have her parents to shelter her from the cold
winds and keep her warm.

Penguins have bodies that are built for the coldest
weather on earth. Their bodies are covered with three
layers of tiny, waterproof feathers, which keep out the
cold wind and keep in their body heat. They also have a
thick layer of fat all over their bodies
to keep them warm.

The penguin family huddles
together. When the sky clears, the
snow will melt. It will be fishing
time again!

A few weeks have passed. Baby Penguin has new feathers. Now she looks like a grown-up. Baby Penguin flaps her flippers. Now she is ready to go somewhere. So are the other penguins. They form a big group near the water.

Baby Penguin follows them. She uses her flippers to slide across the cold ice on her belly.

Baby Penguin quickly discovers that sliding is the best way to get around on the cold snow and ice. Penguins do this by using their fat bellies as toboggans.

Baby Penguin

It is now time for the young penguins' first swim in the sea. Baby Penguin is one of the last little penguins to dive in. She's really swimming fast! Baby Penguin is no longer such a slowpoke!

Tiny Tiger

Written by Jennifer Boudart
Illustrated by Krista Brauckmann-Towns

It is morning in the jungle. Steam rises up from the ground. Jungle plants sparkle with dew. Monkeys and birds chatter in the treetops. It's a morning just like any other morning. Or is it?

Look! Three tiger cubs come tumbling out of their dark cave. Today is their first day outdoors. They are eight weeks old and ready to explore.

The cubs' whiskers twitch as they move through the tall grasses and leaves. A tiger's whiskers are almost as sensitive as fingertips. They help a tiger avoid objects, judge spaces, and feel its way in the dark.

Tiny Tiger

43

The bright sun makes the cubs blink. Their eyes are used to the darkness of the cave. A monkey screams, and two cubs scramble for cover.

The third cub is a little smaller, but much braver, than her brothers. She looks for the noisy monkey swinging through the trees.

Her name is Tiny Tiger, and one day she will grow up to be a beautiful tigress.

Tigers' eyes work well even in low light, so tigers are nocturnal, meaning they are most active at night.

A low grunting sound brings all three cubs running. The cubs know the familiar sound of their mother's voice.

Tiny Tiger and her brothers follow Mother Tiger through the tall jungle grass. Their stripes hide them very well. To other animals, they look like swaying grasses filled with shadows and sunlight.

Every tiger's stripes are unique. A tiger's face markings are so distinctive that they can be used to tell two tigers apart.

Tiny Tiger is amazed by the world around her. There is so much to see, smell, and hear!

Tiny Tiger sees her mother's long, swinging tail. She tries to catch it! Mother holds her tail high out of her baby's reach. Tiny Tiger doesn't use her claws. That would hurt Mother Tiger! Tigers' claws are retractable, which means they can be withdrawn into a tiger's paw like a turtle's head is pulled into its shell.

Tiny Tiger turns to chase her own tail. Round in circles she goes. Her mother grunts softly. Keep moving!

The tiger family comes upon a small lake. It is quiet, cool, and shady—perfect for the hot tigers. First, Mother Tiger checks the area for danger. No jackals or jaguars. Just a few harmless little birds. Mother Tiger heads for the water and her cubs follow her.

The three young tiger cubs have never been swimming. Like all tigers, the three cubs love water. They march right in!

Tigers don't like hot weather. They will often cool themselves off by lying in shallow pools of cool water.

My Little Book of Animal Adventures

The little cubs wrestle and tumble by the cool jungle lake. Tiger cubs play games that are good practice for hunting. They also learn to stalk, chase, and pounce by watching their mother.

Tiny Tiger sees a colorful peacock. She takes a few steps toward the beautiful bird. It flies away! Tiny Tiger thinks the peacock is afraid of her. But she is wrong.

The bird has seen something large in the grass. Suddenly a loud roar freezes Tiny Tiger in her tracks!

There is another tiger here! The cubs run and hide behind their mother. Mother Tiger is not scared because she knows this visitor. He is Father Tiger. They rub necks to say hello.

Tiny Tiger bravely jumps from behind her mother. She growls a baby growl. Her father gently rubs her with his big paw before going on his way.

Tiny Tiger won't always have Mother Tiger to protect her. A tiger cub will leave its mother after two years to find its own territory. There, the cub will spend most of its life hunting and living alone.

Tiny Tiger

Tiny Tiger is a playful cub. She creeps slowly and quietly to practice hunting. Her little body stays low to the ground, and her ears press flat against her head. Suddenly she jumps! She has caught a peacock feather!

One day, Tiny Tiger will catch real food. Tigers are carnivores, meaning they hunt for their food and eat meat. Today is just for fun, though. Her brothers chase her, trying to steal her prize.

Tiny Tiger runs to Mother Tiger and shows her the colorful peacock feather.

The family returns home for a short nap. The cubs cuddle together in front of their cave. Mother Tiger washes each of the three cubs with her rough tongue. Then she lies down with them to rest.

If the cubs try to wander off, Mother Tiger will bring them back. Mother Tiger can carry her cubs by gently grabbing a cub's neck in her mouth. Loose folds of skin on the top of a cub's neck are a natural handle for Mother Tiger.

After her nap, Mother Tiger hunts for food for her little cubs. She leaves them safely napping near the cave.

Tiny Tiger

Tiny Tiger's legs kick as she sleeps. She flicks her tail and growls softly. She dreams of the day when she will grow up to roam the jungle as a mighty tigress.

Baby Pig

Written by Lenaya Raack
Illustrated by Kathy Rusynyk

A pair of big brown eyes peek through the wooden fence in the barn. A young girl kneels in the hay and watches Mother Pig feed her new litter of piglets. The girl stays quiet. She counts the tiny tails—one, two, three . . . all the way up to nine.

The girl gets up and quietly moves around to the other side. Now the girl can see all of the piglets. They are all perfectly pink—except for the littlest one on the end. She has brown spots all over her body. This is the little girl's favorite piglet. She calls her Baby Pig.

Baby Pig

Baby Pig

Baby Pig moves with her family to a new home. It is called a sty or pigpen. It has a fence around it and hay on the ground. Baby Pig lives here with Mother and Father Pig and her sisters and brothers. At night, the piglets sleep close together to stay warm. Sometimes they even sleep on top of one another.

Today, Baby Pig wakes up first. She sniffs the ground looking for food. She is hungry all the time. Suddenly Baby Pig hears the girl coming. Baby Pig watches her pour the food into a long wooden bucket called a trough. Now all of the pigs are awake. Baby Pig has to push past the other hungry pigs to eat.

Today, Baby Pig and her family are going into the barnyard with the other animals. Baby Pig likes the barnyard, because it is much bigger than the sty. There is more room for her to run and play.

The girl opens the gate of the pigpen. One by one, the piglets follow their mother and father into the barnyard. A curious calf comes up to sniff Baby Pig. She doesn't mind. She wants to play, but Mother Pig grunts loudly and the calf moves away.

Baby Pig walks over to the fence, sniffing the ground for food. The girl comes over and says, "Are you hungry, Baby Pig? Here's a treat for you." The little girl gives the pig an apple.

67

Baby Pig

It is summertime on the farm and very hot. The ground is dry and dusty. In the shade of the barn, the chickens roll in the dust to keep their feathers from sticking together. Baby Pig doesn't sweat, so she needs to roll in the mud to get cool.

Soon the girl brings out a hose and makes a big mud hole by squirting water on the dirt. Baby Pig is the first one to jump in. She rolls and wriggles and splashes until she is covered in mud. She's not hot anymore. The other pigs follow Baby Pig. They run and jump into the mud, too. Soon all the pigs are the color of mud. The little girl laughs. "I can hardly see you in all that mud," she says.

Baby Pig is looking for something good to eat. She walks over to where the chickens are eating, but she doesn't want to eat grain. She walks over to where the cows are eating, but she doesn't want to eat hay.

Maybe there is something good to eat in the barn. Baby Pig sticks her head in a pail, but it is empty. She tries to pull her head out, but the pail won't come off! Baby Pig shakes her head, but the pail doesn't move. She begins to run. The chickens and roosters see Baby Pig and run away. The geese see her, too, and honk and fly up on the fence. Splash! Baby Pig lands in the mud. Finally the pail pops off!

Baby Pig

Sometimes, the girl takes Baby Pig for walks. Today, they're going for a short walk down the road. Baby Pig likes to go for walks, because there are lots of new things for her to see. She watches a squirrel run up a tree and a rabbit hop into a bush.

Baby Pig stops to smell the yellow flowers that grow along the road. As they walk farther up the road, they see dogs herding a large flock of sheep. Baby Pig wants to help, but the girl tells her, "No, Baby Pig, pigs don't herd sheep."

Then they stop under an apple tree to rest. The girl feeds Baby Pig an apple for being so good.

Baby Pig is hungry again. This time, Baby Pig tries the corn growing in the field. She squeezes under the fence and races for the big cornstalks. Baby Pig knocks over a cornstalk and eats the ears of corn.

Soon Baby Pig sees a rabbit hopping around the cornstalks and chases it. Baby Pig wants to play, but the rabbit disappears down a hole. Now Baby Pig is lost. The corn is too tall! Baby Pig can't see the barnyard.

Then Baby Pig hears a familiar voice. It's the girl! Baby Pig squeals and the girl comes running to find her.

Baby Pig

Baby Pig is five months old now. She's too big to be picked up and carried by the girl. But she likes to follow the girl around the barnyard while the girl does her chores. She watches as the girl throws grain on the ground and the chickens gobble it up.

Then Baby Pig follows the girl into the barn. The girl climbs up a ladder into the hayloft. She throws hay down to the barn floor to feed the cows. The girl doesn't notice the hay falling on top of Baby Pig. Baby Pig is covered in hay. When the girl sees the pig in the hay, she giggles playfully and says, "Sorry, Baby Pig."

The farm is quiet. It is nighttime now. In the barn, the cows sleepily eat one last mouthful of hay. The calves are already asleep in their stalls. The hens are sitting on their nests in the hen house. Their chicks are safely tucked under their mothers' feathers. Outside, the pigs are back in their sty. They are lying down and getting ready to sleep, too.

The barnyard is dark and empty now. The farmhouse is quiet. Baby Pig and the girl sit on the bottom step of the porch. They watch the fireflies blinking on and off in the darkness. When it is time for bed, the girl walks Baby Pig back to her pen and gives her a good-night hug.

Baby Pig

Now Baby Pig is one year old. Soon she will have her own babies. Every day the girl brings food and stops to talk to her.

When the new piglets are born, the girl chooses one to be her new pet. She knows this piglet is just as special as Baby Pig.

Bear Cub

Written by Sarah Toast
Illustrated by Krista Brauckmann-Towns

As summer draws to an end, Mother Bear roams through the mountain forest, gathering and eating enormous amounts of berries and fruit.

Mother Bear is putting on fat so she can sleep in her den the entire winter. The layer of fat will keep her warm and help her provide rich milk for the baby bear that will be born.

The air is turning cold. Mother Bear must hurry. She still has a lot of work to do. She must find a home for herself and her baby.

Bear Cub

Bear Cub

Mother Bear chooses a rocky cave to be her den during the winter. Inside the den, she and her baby will be protected from the cold wind and blowing snow. She pads it with moss, leaves, and grass to make it warm and soft for herself and the new baby.

As the first flakes of winter snow begin to fall, Mother Bear settles down and drifts off to sleep.

Soon the falling snow will build up outside and close off the den, keeping Mother Bear and her baby safe from harm.

In the middle of winter, when the snow drifts are deep outside the den, Mother Bear's tiny cub is born. With closed eyes and hardly any fur, the cub will grow quickly, nourished by Mother Bear's rich milk.

Baby Bear and Mother Bear sleep on, but Mother Bear will wake up and protect him if the winter home is disturbed.

Mother Bear sits or lies on her side in her den and keeps her cub warm by cuddling him close to her warm body.

Bear Cub

Bear Cub

In a few weeks, Baby Bear's eyes open. He is now covered in thick, soft fur. Mother Bear and Baby Bear stay in their snug den another month.

Bear cubs will stay in the den for three months before they venture outside. During these three months, they spend most of their time sleeping. They wake only to drink their mother's milk.

In the spring, Baby Bear and his mother emerge from the den. Mother Bear shows Baby Bear how to look through the forest for tender shoots that will make a good meal.

Mother Bear makes her way with Baby Bear
down the grassy slope to the elk's winter range. She lifts
up her head and sniffs the breeze. Baby Bear moves
his raised head back and forth so hard that he falls
right over.

Bears have such small eyes that people often
assume they also have poor eyesight, but bears probably
see as well as most humans.

Mother Bear finds an elk
that died in the winter when the
snows were deep and not enough
food could be found.

90

Bear Cub

Mother Bear eats as much as she can of the nourishing elk meat. Then she carefully buries it in a shallow hole and covers it with leaves, twigs, and dirt. She will return to it later.

Baby Bear learns by watching what his mother does. The most important rules for Baby Bear to learn are to follow Mother, obey Mother, and have fun.

Bear cubs stay with their mother about two years. During this time, they learn many survival tips, such as what to eat and how to escape danger, before they venture out on their own.

Mother Bear teaches her baby cub to turn over fallen branches and look for grubs to eat. With their long, sharp claws, Baby Bear and Mother Bear dig up bulbs, roots, and snails.

Bears will eat almost anything they can get their paws on, including grasses, berries, tree bark, plants, insects, some small mammals, and, of course, sweet honey!

When his mother stops to rest, Baby Bear likes to play. He climbs all over her. He somersaults into her lap and nibbles her ears, then runs off to chase a tiny field mouse.

Bear Cub

Bear Cub

When Mother Bear looks up from playing with her cub, she sees that a lean wolf is watching her and Baby Bear. Quickly she chases the cub into a hollow tree stump. Then she turns to face the wolf.

Mother Bear stands up on her hind legs, swings her front paws, and roars a loud growl. The wolf runs away.

Bears have five claws on each foot. They use their front paws for catching and holding prey, digging for insects and roots, and climbing trees.

Mother Bear calls to her cub, but he doesn't come out of the hollow stump. Mother Bear goes to find out why.

Baby Bear has found a treat. It is a honeycomb with honey from last summer still inside. Baby Bear sticks his little paw in the honeycomb and then licks it. He tastes the wildflowers of summer in the sweet honey.

As Baby Bear's first summer draws to an end, he is able to find his own food, although he might drink milk from Mother Bear occasionally. Now he must eat as much food as he can to prepare for his winter sleep.

Bear Cub

97

When Baby Bear backs out of the hollow log, he brings some tasty honeycomb for his mother. She happily eats the honey, and then she and her cub give each other a true bear hug.

Baby Dolphin

Written by Sarah Toast
Illustrated by Gary Torrisi

In the warm waters near the shore, a small herd of bottlenose dolphins plays among the waves. Two leap together high into the air, then they arc and dive in. Two other dolphins ride the surf on an incoming wave.

The dolphins move their tail fins up and down to gain speed. They use their flippers to make sharp turns and quick stops.

Dolphins can swim as fast as 23 miles per hour, and they can jump ten feet into the air.

Baby Dolphin

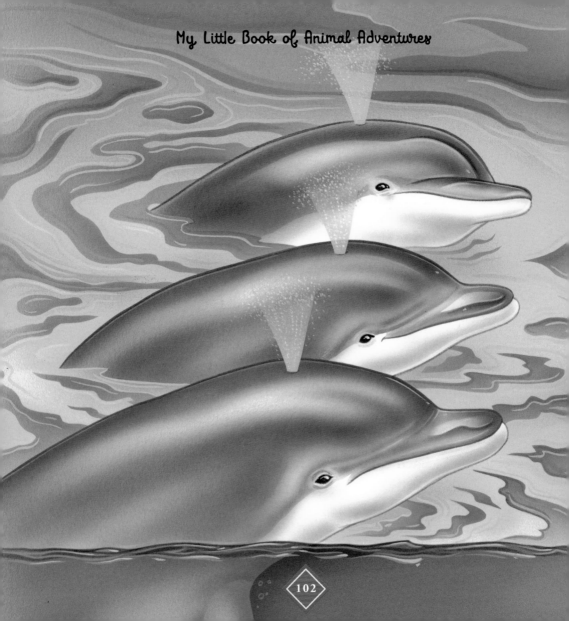

Baby Dolphin

A small group of dolphins hunting for fish comes up and "blows" together. The dolphin in the front is Mother Dolphin. She must go to the surface to breathe through her blowhole.

Dolphins are mammals which means they breathe air out of blowholes on the tops of their heads. They return to the surface for air about four times each minute.

Dolphins find fish by making clicking sounds and listening to the echoes that bounce back. The dolphins can talk to each other by whistling and calling.

Mother Dolphin and two other adult dolphins find a school of small fish in the shallow water of a bay. The dolphins rush at the fish.

The fish are swept up in the wave and pushed ahead of the speeding dolphins. They land on the sandy shore. The three dolphins snap up the fish and slide back into the water.

Dolphins may look like fish, too, but they are really warm-blooded mammals. They breathe air from the surface, give birth to live young, and nurse their young with milk.

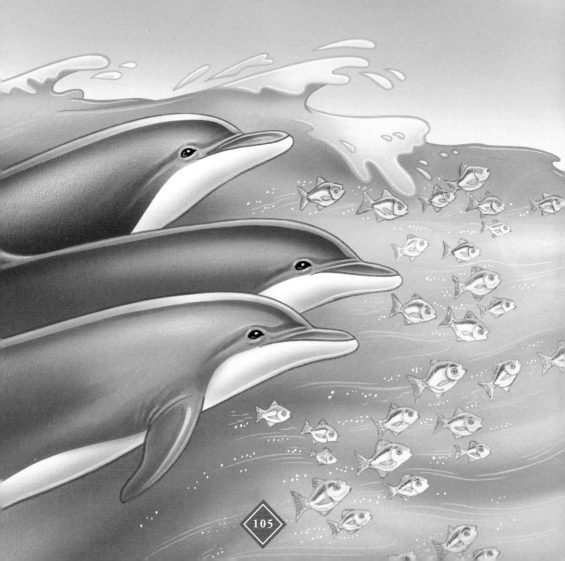

106

Baby Dolphin

Soon Mother Dolphin will be ready to give birth to her baby. She has help from two dolphin "aunties," who stay next to her. Other dolphins from the herd gather around them and whistle softly.

As soon as Baby Dolphin is born, the two helpers guide her to the surface of the water for her very first breath. After she breathes, Baby Dolphin can float.

Dolphins have their own underwater language of sounds, clicks, and whistles. They use these sounds to communicate with each other and the environment.

Mother Dolphin nurses her hungry Baby Dolphin near the surface of the calm ocean water. Mother Dolphin floats on her side and squirts her extra-rich milk into her baby's waiting mouth.

Baby Dolphin floats near the surface so she can breathe while she is fed. The "aunties" stay nearby and encourage the mother and baby with soft sounds.

Mother Dolphin will nurse Baby Dolphin for a long time. As Baby Dolphin gets older, she will eat fish, shrimp, and squid.

Baby Dolphin

Mother Dolphin stays beside her baby throughout the summer. The "aunties" also take care of Baby Dolphin.

Baby Dolphin is very playful and curious. She can swim well and loves to nudge her mother. Baby Dolphin is growing fast. Soon she will grow a thick layer of blubber like her mother. It will help her float and keep her warm.

Baby Dolphin is getting tired after playing so much. At night, she sleeps just below the surface of the water like the other dolphins.

Baby Dolphin is quick to learn each dolphin's unique whistle. The dolphins in the herd also bark, click, moan, and mew to keep in touch with one another and express their feelings.

Dolphins have no vocal chords, but they can produce sounds with a special oil-filled organ in their foreheads called the melon. These sounds come out of their blowholes.

The dolphins work together to take care of Baby Dolphin and the other young dolphins. They cooperate in feeding and defending the herd.

The dolphins are all spread out when a shark swims close to their group. Grown-up dolphins quickly surround Baby Dolphin and all the other young ones to protect them.

Dolphins always travel in small schools, or groups, to protect themselves against predators.

Suddenly four other grown dolphins rush toward the menacing shark. The adult dolphins ram it hard with their beaks, lifting it clear out of the water.

The shark flees, but some of the dolphins are exhausted and hurt. They help lift each other to the surface so they can rest and breathe through their blowholes.

The danger is gone, but Baby Dolphin stays close to the older dolphins. Baby Dolphin floats up with Mother Dolphin to take a breath of fresh air and rest for a short time.

If dolphins can protect themselves against their enemies like the shark, they can live a long time. Some dolphins live up to 35 years in the wild.

After the dolphins have rested, they celebrate by playing games in the warm water. Baby Dolphin flips through the air and uses her tail to splash her friends.

Duckling

Written by Sarah Toast
Illustrated by Judith Love

It is summer, and Mother Duck is making a nest. In a clump of reeds near the edge of the pond, Mother Duck finds a hollow place in the ground. She lines it with grass and soft cattail stems.

Mother Duck lays her nine smooth eggs. She plucks soft feathers from her breast to line the nest and protect the eggs.

Inside each egg is a tiny growing duck. It is attached to a bag of thick, yellow liquid called yolk. Yolk is special food for the growing duck.

Duckling

121

Mother Duck sits on her eggs for many days and nights. Whenever she leaves the nest, she covers her eggs with a soft blanket of down to hide them and keep them warm.

At last Mother Duck hears the "pip-pip" of her ducklings working to get out of their shells. The last little duckling to break out of its shell is called Dabble.

Baby ducklings peck their way out by using a special egg tooth. Located on the tip of the beak, this egg tooth will fall off later.

Mother Duck protects her new ducklings by rubbing her tummy feathers over them in the nest. Now the ducklings are waterproof. They will stay warm and dry when they swim.

Mother Duck can waterproof her own feathers by combing oil into them with her bill. The oil that she uses comes from a place near her tail.

When ducks rub this oil over their feathers, it is called preening. The oil hardens and the feathers become waxy, allowing the water to roll right off.

Duckling

125

While the ducklings are resting in their nest, a skunk comes to the water's edge for a drink. Mother Duck and the ducklings try to stay really still and quiet so the skunk will not notice them.

Mother Duck's spotted brown feathers and the stripes on her ducklings blend in with the tall grasses and reeds.

The ducklings will stay very close to their mother until they can fly. It usually takes about two months before they learn to fly.

Dabble is a special type of duck known as a dabbler duck. She sees Mother Duck taking good care of her brothers and sisters. She knows that her mother will take good care of her, too.

The tiny ducklings are only a few hours old, but they can run. They follow their mother down to the water's edge for their very first swim.

Ducklings can usually swim right after they are born. But they must wait for their mother to waterproof their feathers before they can take their first swim.

Dabble is the very first young duckling to jump into the water after Mother Duck. Her sisters and brothers gleefully jump in after her. They bob on the water like balls of fluff.

What a glorious and fun pond! Suddenly Dabble is dazzled by a dragonfly that lands on a nearby lily pad. A colorful butterfly grabs her attention next. Then she stares at a caterpillar on a cattail leaf.

Now Dabble is getting quite hungry, and she knows exactly what to do. She tips up her tail and stretches her bill down to the muddy bottom of the pond to find plenty of plants, roots, and seeds.

Dabble enjoys dipping down to look for food underwater, then popping up again to see where Mother Duck is.

Dabbling is what Dabble does when she turns upside down to look for food underwater. Only her tail can be seen above the water.

There is plenty of food now, but in the winter ducks can't find insects, seeds, or plants to eat. So every fall, they fly south in a "V" formation. The weather is warm there, and they will find plenty of food.

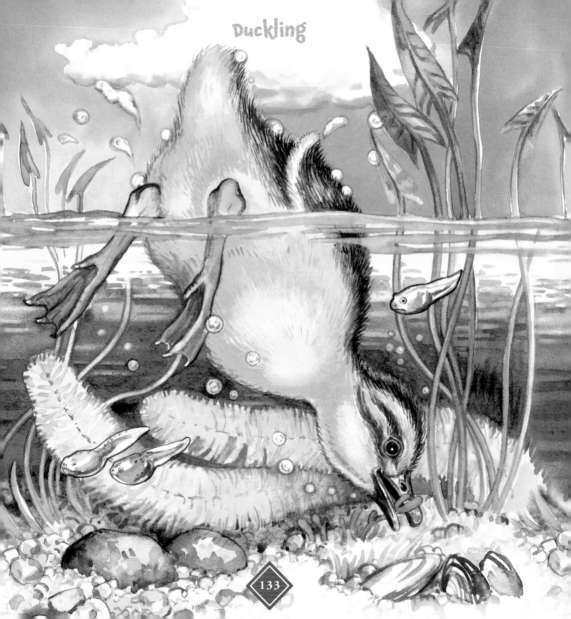

Duckling

Dabble watches a colorful butterfly flitting among the reeds in the pond. Then Dabble dips down to enjoy another nibble. She lifts her tiny head to quack hello to a red-winged blackbird.

Mother Duck dips down to get something to eat for herself. Underwater, Mother Duck sees a big snapping turtle swimming toward her little ducklings.

Just as quick as a quack, Mother Duck calls out for her ducklings to return to shore, but Dabble is underwater and doesn't hear her.

Mother Duck swims swiftly over to Dabble and gets between Dabble and the snapping turtle. Dabble pops up and swims to shore with Mother Duck, and the turtle swims away.

A duck's three front toes are webbed and used as paddles to swim really fast through the water and away from snapping turtles.

Mother Duck will do anything to protect her ducklings. Sometimes she will even flap her wings and quack loudly to scare an enemy away.

Duckling

That night all the ducklings sleep warm and safe in the nest after their busy first day in the world. Dabble is dreaming of tomorrow, when she will see the bright butterfly again.

Panda Baby

Written by Sarah Toast
Illustrated by Debbie Pinkney

It is late in the summer in the steep and rocky mountains of China. In the mist of twilight, Mother Panda stirs.

Mother Panda leaves her den to climb farther down the side of the mountain. She follows long paths and tunnels that connect her den with the feeding places where she will eat bamboo all through the night.

Pandas are one of the world's rarest animals. There are approximately 1,000 left living in the wild.

Panda Baby

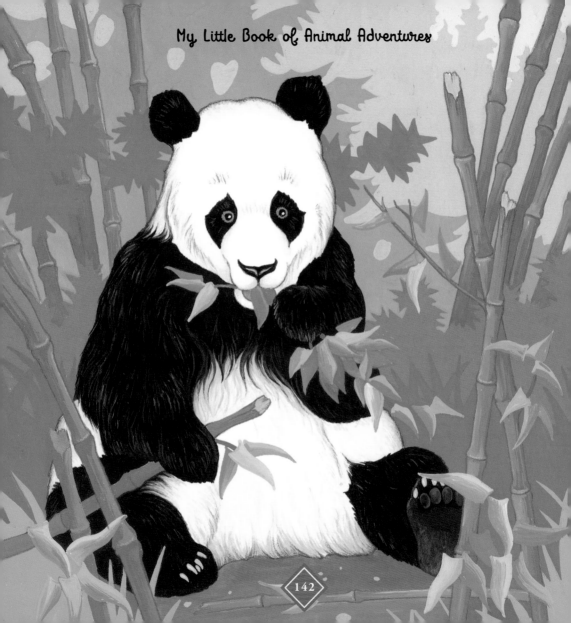

My Little Book of Animal Adventures

Panda Baby

Mother Panda wanders in the cool, damp mist through bamboo thickets sheltered by evergreen trees. She is always looking for good places to eat.

Mother Panda has an extra "thumb" that helps her handle the bamboo leaves, stems, and shoots with great care. Mother Panda spends most of her time eating the tough bamboo.

Pandas eat more than just bamboo. They also like to eat honey and mushrooms. But bamboo is their main source of food.

Panda bears are not able to digest bamboo very well, so they must eat up to sixty pounds of bamboo a day to get the energy they need.

To find this much bamboo, Mother Panda roams over a lot of ground day and night looking for good feeding places. That's why she has several dens and places to sleep.

Pandas don't have much free time, because they spend so much time eating all of this bamboo. They spend up to 16 hours a day eating bamboo!

Panda Baby

Panda Baby

In the gray dawn, Mother Panda climbs back up the side of the mountain and enters her cave. There she gives birth to her tiny baby. Panda Baby is pink, with only a small amount of fur. His eyes are closed, but he has a loud squeal.

A baby panda is very small when it is just born. It weighs only five ounces and could be held in a human's hand!

Mother Panda cradles Panda Baby against her chest with her large forepaws. She has a lot to do now that Panda Baby has arrived.

Mother Panda stays inside the den with her baby. She nurses Panda Baby, but for several days she does not go out to find food for herself.

A mother panda cradles her cub constantly for the first month of its life.

In only a month, Panda Baby has the same warm fur coat as his mother. Not long after that, his eyes open. From then on, Mother Panda can take her cub out of the den.

When Panda Baby is full-grown, he could weigh 350 pounds and measure five feet long.

Panda Baby

Panda Baby

Mother Panda will carry her baby with her everywhere for a long time. Mother Panda can carry her cub using her mouth. She gently picks him up and is very careful to make sure that little Panda Baby won't fall.

It is late in the autumn when Panda Baby learns to stand up. In early winter, Panda Baby is finally able to run and play.

Soon after its first birthday, a young panda will leave its mother to find its own territory and its own bamboo supply.

Mother Panda and Panda Baby roam the bamboo groves to find enough food for the hungry mother. While his mother eats, Panda Baby clowns and plays in the leaves. He isn't old enough to eat bamboo yet.

Mother Panda and her baby search through the forest for comfortable places to rest in hollow trees, caves, and other rocky places.

When Panda Baby is older, he will spend most of his life alone in a small territory. A panda marks its territory by rubbing the scent glands near its back legs against trees. Sometimes a panda marks a tree while standing on its head!

Panda Baby

Panda Baby

Mother Panda and her baby will climb down the mountain as winter gets colder. They will not sleep through the winter like some bears do.

Bamboo stays green all year round, so Mother Panda will be able to find plenty to eat during the winter. Mother Panda will continue to nurse Panda Baby for many more months.

In winter the bamboo forests are covered in snow, but pandas don't mind. Their large, round bodies keep in the heat, and their thick fur coats keep them dry.

Panda Baby is getting bigger and stronger. He goes with his mother on longer walks up and down the side of the mountain and through the dense forest. They wade across streams and swim in rivers. And they climb trees.

Pandas are good at climbing trees. But they're not so good at climbing down. They come down headfirst, and sometimes they land with a thud!

The first snow of winter will soon fall. After a day of playing and exploring, Panda Baby rests in his den.

Panda Baby

Panda Baby

Panda Baby wakes up to his first snowfall. He loves the cold snowflakes! Panda Baby wakes Mother Panda and then does a handspring to show his delight.